A Girl Called Dog

By Nicola Davies

Illustrated by James de la Rue

CORGI BOOKS

For Eva and Libby,
and with thanks to VB and LW.

RENFREWSHIRE COUNCIL	
179865121	
Bertrams	18/07/2011
	£5.99
LOC	

Chapter 1

Dog wasn't really a dog, she was a human girl, but she was called Dog because that is what Uncle had always called her.

Uncle had brought Dog to live in his pet shop so long ago that she didn't remember anywhere else. She felt she had always lived amongst the cages of mice and hamsters, rabbits and budgies; eating the same food as they did and sleeping in the storeroom at the back of the shop, on an old pet bed.

It was Dog's job to look after all the pets, and Uncle's job to sit by the till eating sausages and reading the paper. When anyone came into the shop, Dog had to hide because if anyone saw her, anyone at all, Uncle said, she would be taken away.

"You'll be put in a black, black box," he told her, "and that will be the end of you!"

Uncle reminded her of this every day, opening the box he kept under the till so she could see the darkness inside, then slamming it shut so that the lock clicked; the sound made Dog shudder.

So, when customers came, Dog crouched on her bed, trembling; even when the shop was empty she kept away from the door and the windows, just in case. All she ever saw of the world outside was the weak sunlight that struggled through the dirty glass of the pet-shop window and fell on the floor between the sacks of Pussy Poo cat litter.

Uncle had a fat, angry face and a mouth that didn't smile. Luckily he was very tall, so Dog hardly ever had to look further than his knees.

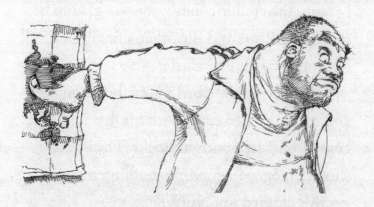

He had two moods: good and bad. When he was in a good mood, he ate sausages with his fingers, and pointed at the map above the till with a greasy finger and told Dog: "The blue part is the ocean and the green part is land. So don't *say* I haven't given you an educayshun. But you can't *say* anything, can you, you dumb little mongrel!" And then he'd laugh, and bits of sausage would spray all over the shop.

Dog didn't care that he laughed at her because she couldn't speak; she was glad to be quiet, like Esme and the other animals, not full of shouty words like Uncle.

When he was in a bad mood, he stomped and raged, dented cages with his fists and split bags of bird seed with his kicks. Then he'd shout, "Dog, you good-for-nothing mongrel, get this cleaned up! NOW!"

But in spite of Uncle, Dog felt lucky. She didn't have to live in a cage like the pets she cared for or watch her friends being sold as they did. Dog's best friend was Esme the coati. Esme had a slender, inquisitive nose and a long stripy tail, with a short, cosy little body in between. She had lived at the shop for as long as Dog could remember and her fur was getting thin; there were even a few bald patches here and there. No one, Dog thought happily, would choose Esme instead of a baby bunny or a little mouse!

Esme was too clever to live in a cage, so she followed Dog everywhere, helping with the animals by checking that all their food tasted good. Her favourite thing (apart from fresh grapes and sliced banana) was sitting on Dog's shoulders, with her tail wrapped around Dog's neck. They shared sausage scraps when Uncle was in a good mood, and when he wasn't, Esme hid her nose in Dog's hair and breathed warmth onto her head.

Chapter 2

Uncle's bad moods were happening more and more. They were keeping people out of the pet shop. Sometimes, whole days went by without Dog having to go to the storeroom so as not to be seen and taken away in a black, black box. The baby rabbits all grew up and some of the mice began to get quite old.

Late one winter afternoon, when Uncle had smashed an empty goldfish bowl in a temper because there had been no customers at all for three days, the bell over the shop door suddenly rang out. Just in time, Dog and Esme dived behind some sacks of cat litter, then peeped out through a gap. If Uncle sold something, it often changed his mood from bad to good.

However, instead of a customer, a skinny postman struggled over to the counter with a huge parcel, wrapped in brown paper and tied with a spider's web of coloured string.

"Delivery!" he said with a big smile, putting the parcel down on the counter in front of Uncle.

"Didn't order nothing," Uncle growled without looking up from his crisps.

The postman stopped smiling. "But it's addressed to you from the Government Pest Disposal Unit," he said, nervously reading the label. "It's an official parcel."

"Don't care," said Uncle. "I don't want it."

He flattened the crisp packet with a noise that made the postman jump. His face was bright, bright red.

Esme wound her tail round Dog's arm for comfort; the last time Uncle's face had been that colour, he'd smashed the budgie cage and cracked the mouse tank.

"I don't care who sent it," Uncle bellowed. "Take it away!"

The postman turned pale under his peaked cap. In a very small voice he said, "No!" and fled through the door, leaving the bell jumping wildly on its spring.

Dog and Esme stayed in their hiding place

while Uncle stamped about the shop shouting,
"Delivery! I'll give you delivery! I didn't order
anything!" He pushed the parcel off the
counter and gave it a good kick. But there was
something very hard under the brown paper;
Uncle yelped with pain and sat down.

"Dog!" he yelped. "Dog! Get out here."

Uncle this angry was dangerous. Dog made Esme stay behind the sacks and slunk out to the front of the shop.

"Sort that parcel out!" Uncle screamed. Dog concentrated on the floor and got ready to dodge a kick. But suddenly Uncle's anger went down like a soggy balloon. He limped over to the door and turned the sign to CLOSED. "I'm going upstairs," he growled, "and I don't want any disturbing. All right?"

Dog shut her eyes, and nodded hard. When she looked again, he'd gone. She heard his footsteps going up the stairs to the flat above the shop. A moment after that, the sound of the TV came through the floorboards. Esme came out from behind the sacks and pushed her nose into Dog's hand: they knew that once Uncle had his telly on, they were all safe for the night.

Chapter 3

Dog walked all around the parcel and took a good look at it. There was a row of pictures of animals – an ant, a dog, a small bird and a snake, all of them with big red crosses through them. She didn't need to be able to read the words beside the picture to understand what the "Government Pest Disposal Unit" was for. There would be something dead inside the box and she would have to sort it out, as Uncle had ordered. But not now, because this was her favourite part of the day and she didn't want to spoil it with something dead.

With Uncle safely snoring in front of his

TV, Dog could give all the animals a little
freedom. She opened the cages, and slowly
all the small prisoners came out into the faint
light that shone in from the streetlamp.
There was no hurrying or scurrying. Most
of the animals didn't even stray very far from
their cage. The budgies did a few circuits,
then perched on the counter in a row to
preen and gossip. The mice and rats wandered
about for a while, then settled down to groom
their fur, or chew thoughtfully on a bit of
saved supper. Nobody looked for a way to
escape. For Dog, Esme and everyone else, it
was just nice to be out of reach of Uncle's
bad temper for a while and enjoy a little peace
and quiet.

Squuuuaaaawwwwkk! Squawk!

The loudest sound that Dog had ever heard
was coming from the box! Whatever was in

there was definitely not dead. All the animals froze in shock. At once, the TV upstairs fell silent and Uncle's footsteps crossed the floor. If Uncle came down and found everyone out, free in the shop, Dog didn't want to imagine what might happen.

Squuuuaaaawwwkkk! The sound came again, even louder than before. Tiny feet pattered and wings fluttered as all the animals fled towards their cages. Even with everyone back behind bars, Dog knew that Uncle would still be furious at being disturbed and she would be blamed, because she hadn't "sorted out" the strange parcel.

Dog rushed over to the box. Whatever it was inside, it must be made to shut up. Frantically she ripped away the string and paper. The box had fallen so that the lid was at the side. Dog pulled at it, and Esme scrabbled at the edge, trying to lever it up with her long claws. From upstairs there were the unmistakable sounds of Uncle getting ready to come down! Then, suddenly, with a sigh and creak, the lid lifted and a cloud of sawdust spilled onto the pet-shop floor. In the middle of it, something was flailing about, making that terrible, terrible noise, louder still now without the box to muffle it.

Squuuuaaaawwwwkk! Squawk!

Desperate to make it shut up, Dog simply jumped on the whatever it was, pinning it to the floor. It gave one last *Scrreeeeeeech!* and was silent. Dog lay there with sawdust up her nose and in her eyes, listening. Footsteps came to the top of the stairs, then stopped. There was a pause that seemed to last for hours. All the animals held their breath . . . The footsteps retreated, the TV blared out again.

They were safe!

The sawdust settled, and in the glimmer from beyond the pet-shop window, Dog could finally see what she had caught. A single furious eye stared up at her, and below that, a huge curved beak. Esme realized what it was at once and, with a contemptuous snuffle, wheezed off to bed. She didn't like birds of any sort, especially not big ones, and this one was big. Very big. A huge parrot – a macaw, in fact, almost as long from beak to tail as Dog was tall. It had big feet, with sharp claws. What with those and the beak, Dog realized that it could have hurt her very badly, and yet it hadn't.

The bird sneezed, and some sawdust fell

off its body. In the dim light it was impossible to see what colour its feathers were, but it was plain that there weren't many of them. There were patches of bare skin, just a few feathers in the tail, and the wings were so ragged that Dog doubted if the bird would be able to fly. No one, she thought disgustedly, had looked after this bird for a very, very long time!

The bird turned to look at her with both its eyes. It didn't seem angry at all any more. It opened its beak, but this time it wasn't a scream that came out but a much, much quieter and more surprising sound. "*Hungry!*" said the bird. "*Very!*"

Its voice wasn't human – more like an un-oiled hinge – but it had clearly spoken. Dog had never heard of creatures speaking, and it startled her so much that she dropped the bird immediately. This proved that it definitely couldn't fly, because it stayed sprawled on the floor in a tangle of wings.

"*Ow, ow, ow,*" it cried. "*Hurted me!*"

It lay there, flapping weakly and waving its legs in the air, then went quite still.

"*Help!*" it said rather sadly. "*Help. Please.*"

Talking or not, here was a being that needed her care. Dog gently gathered the huge parrot up in her arms. In spite of its length it was terribly light and there seemed to be no strength in the big feet and long wings.

"*Hungry, very,*" it said. "*Very, very.*"

Chapter 4

Carefully Dog carried the bird to the store room and put it on the table. It lay quietly while she lit a candle in a jar and fetched some fruit from the pets' larder. Uncle wouldn't notice if she used a few extra bits.

The sound of chopping attracted Esme's attention. She sat staring at the bird, taking long sniffs of it with her wavering snout. But when Dog stopped her stealing slices of apple and banana, she snorted crossly and went back to bed.

Dog fed the macaw and dripped water into its beak. After it had eaten four and a half bananas and two apples, it sat up and wobbled a little back and forth.

"*Sleeeeeep!*" it said, then belched and closed its eyes.

Dog put a ring of jumbo cans of Happee Kittee around the bird to stop it falling over in the night, blew out the candle and went to bed.

She sat on the old blanket beside Esme, but Esme was still cross; she bristled her fur and turned her back. Dog shrugged and lay down anyway. Just as she closed her eyes and felt the warmth of sleep slipping over her . . .

"*C-c-c-cold!*" said the bird from the table.

Dog got up and relit the candle. The parrot was shivering so much that the cans of cat food had begun to rattle.

It was cold in the storeroom where Dog and Esme slept. There wasn't another blanket to wrap the bird in – she would have to improvise. Dog cut the bird a jacket of newspaper, found some string and wrapped it around its body, leaving its feet free. But still the bird shivered. It was so weak, Dog thought that it might die of cold without extra warmth to get it through the night.

She laid the parrot down gently in the middle of her own bed, where it could sleep between her and Esme and be warmer. This was not to Esme's liking: she snorted, got up and went to curl in the corner, on a pile of newspapers.

Dog lay in the dark, trying to fit herself around the bird's awkward long body, and listening to the sound of her friend's angry paper-scrunching.

"*C-c-c-cold*," whispered the bird. Dog was quite cold herself now with this spiky parcel of parrot to sleep with instead of nice, cosy Esme. She was just thinking she would never get to sleep when there was a *tick-tack*, *tick-tack* of coati claws on the concrete floor, and Esme's nose pushed comfortably under her arm. Esme settled her warm body into the small of Dog's back and sighed contentedly. Dear Esme, she never stayed cross for long. Dog pulled the parrot a little closer. It stopped shivering and rustled sleepily in its newsprint coat.

"*Night night!*" it said, and then, almost at once, began to snore.

Chapter 5

Dog woke up to the sound of someone whispering urgently in her ear. She opened her eyes and there was the parrot, its paper jacket ripped to shreds and its scrappy wings free. It was clear that a good supper and a night's rest had done it a lot of good. It certainly didn't look ready to die any more!

It climbed onto her chest, put its beak close to her face, and whispered again. "*Poo!*" it said. "*Poo.*"

Dog wasn't sure what it wanted. The budgies never had any trouble pooing anywhere, everywhere! In fact she often had to spend quite a while cleaning up after their evening exercise. Perhaps the remaining bit of jacket was getting in the parrot's way, but when she tried to help the bird out of it, it pushed her hand away impatiently and began to march about on the concrete saying, "*Poo, poo, poo,*" more and more loudly.

Dog couldn't think what was wrong, and Esme was no help. She liked quiet in the morning. She shoved her head under the blanket and went back to sleep.

Perhaps the bird was house-trained, Dog thought. She rushed to find a litter tray and some Pussy Poo, and brought it to the very agitated bird. But all it did was snatch the corner of the tray in its curved beak and turn it upside down.

"*No!*" said the bird crossly. "*Poo! Poo!*" And then it made an unmistakable watery whooshing noise, copying the sound so perfectly that Dog knew at once what the bird wanted. She picked it up and ran to the other side of the shop, where a little door led to the customer WC which Uncle allowed her to use.

"*Yes!*" said the bird.

Dog lifted it up, and it held onto the edge of the slippery plastic seat with its claws. Immediately it poked its bottom over the space and sighed. The biggest, longest poo that Dog had ever seen from a bird dropped into the water with a huge *splash!* She began to laugh. The sound bubbled from her tummy and welled up to her head. It brought Esme running from her late bed. She climbed on Dog's shoulders and wrapped her tail around Dog's neck in sheer delight.

The parrot flattened its feathers and looked away from them. "*Rude,*" it said. "*Very.*"

Then it lost its grip on the lavatory seat and had to be rescued from disappearing down the bowl. Still laughing, Dog carried it to the storeroom and left it with a bowl of fruit and some budgie seed so that it could recover its dignity in peace.

Chapter 6

Mornings were busy. There was everyone's breakfast to get, and all the cages had to be cleaned out. And this morning Dog had lost time over the parrot's toilet arrangements. Esme tried to help with the usual chores but she kept being distracted by bits of grape and stray peanuts. So Dog hadn't even started on clearing up the mess that the parrot's box had left behind when she heard Uncle's heavy footsteps on the stairs.

As Uncle came into the shop, she crouched over the sawdust and bits of string, trying to hide the fact that she hadn't sorted it out.

But Uncle saw. He came and stood right over her. Even without looking up, Dog knew how red his face was getting.

"I thought I told you to sort that box out," he said. Dog answered by sweeping the sawdust even faster than before, but Uncle kicked the brush out of her hands. Dog kept very still, staring at his big, heavy feet.

"When I tell you to do something, I expect—" But Uncle didn't get the chance to finish, because his own voice began to call loudly from the storeroom.

"*Dog! Dog!*" said the voice, exactly the way Uncle had called out last night.

Uncle turned angrily towards the sound. "What's going on?" he growled.

There, waddling carefully over the floor, trailing strands of newspaper and string behind it, was the macaw. "*Delivery? Delivery?*" it said with Uncle's voice. "*I'll give you delivery!*"

Dog's heart raced with fear. There was no way to protect the bird from Uncle's anger, and surely this would make him very, very angry indeed.

Uncle staggered back and sat down heavily on the sacks of Pussy Poo. The parrot stood at his feet, still speaking his words, in his voice. But instead of getting angry, Uncle just stared and stared at the bird. "You," he told it at last, "are going to make me a fortune!"

"*A fortune!*" said the parrot. "*A fortune!*"

Chapter 7

Word spread about the talking parrot that could imitate any voice or any sound the first time it heard it. People came from all over the city to see it, and to hear their own voices coming out of a bird's beak. The pet shop got more customers in a day than it used to get in a year. People were pleased to buy pets from the shop with the amazing parrot. Very soon all the mice and rats, the rabbits and budgies were sold, and Uncle was making so much money from charging people to see the parrot that he didn't bother to get any more animals.

At the start of every day he made Dog tie

the parrot's feet to a perch at the front of the shop so it could only move one pace to each side. Dog hated this cruel confinement. One morning she tried to give the bird a longer leash so it could move about more freely, but when Uncle spotted that, he slapped Dog hard.

That night, when Dog undid the parrot's feet to return it to its cage, the big macaw leaned towards her ear and whispered, in its own raspy voice, "*Carlos.*"

To begin with Dog didn't understand, but then the bird fixed her first with one bright eye and then the other.

"*Carlos,*" it whispered again, and Dog knew that it – he – was introducing himself to her. She nodded at him and smiled, knowing, with a strange little turn of her heart, that Esme was no longer her only friend.

Uncle called the parrot Polly, but now Dog knew his real name. All day long "Polly" had to sit on his perch, while strings of gawping people queued up to say stupid things and hear the parrot say them right back.

"Pretty Polly" was the favourite, of course, and Carlos had to repeat it a hundred times a

32

day, in a hundred different tones and accents. He mimicked other sounds too – the ring of the shop doorbell, the sound of a wrapper being taken from a chocolate bar, a baby wailing. Dog felt sure Carlos was just trying not to get too bored with the endless "Pretty Polly"s.

Hard-worked and bored though he was, Carlos was at least well fed. Customers didn't like to see a thin, scruffy macaw, even if it could mirror their every sound. Uncle bought exotic fruits and nuts for Dog to feed him (although a few found their way to Esme). Soon the straggly feathers and the bare skin had disappeared and the bird was covered in beautiful plumage – deep turquoise blue over its back and a golden yellow on its belly.

Dog was glad that Carlos was beautiful again, but otherwise life grew gloomy. Uncle extended his opening hours, and with so many customers, Dog spent most of her time hidden in the storeroom. In the few moments when the shop was empty, Uncle would call her out so she could clean up the crisp packets, sweet papers and drink cans that the trail of visitors had left behind. Worst of all, during the day Esme was put in a cage, because she had nipped the finger of a little boy who had pulled her tail. All day long, Uncle amused himself by poking her with pencils or rattling the bars of her cage.

The only time life was bearable was after Uncle had gone upstairs to bed. Then Esme could come out of her cage, and Dog would groom her thin fur. Dog groomed Carlos too, scratching the top of his head as he closed his eyes with pleasure. Then the three of them would eat whatever was left of Carlos's rations. Dog peeled the mangoes and gave them each a slice; Carlos cracked Brazil nuts in his beak and didn't mind sharing. Esme seemed to forget that Carlos was a bird and began to treat him more like an odd kind of coati.

Weeks turned into months. Each night, Uncle spent longer and longer counting more and more money. He bought an extra-strong cage and made Dog lock Carlos in it as soon as the shop was closed, then give the key back to Uncle. The three friends' cosy evenings just weren't the same with prison bars in the way.

Esme's fur began to come out in handfuls and Carlos looked more and more exhausted. At night none of them seemed to have the appetite for mangoes or Brazil nuts any more. Dog did what she could for her friends, but she was just as miserable as they were.

Chapter 8

Just when Dog imagined that things couldn't get any worse, worse happened. She was dozing in the storeroom, near to closing time, when she heard a customer start to bargain with Uncle.

"I'll give you a tenner," he said, "for the funny-looking beast with the long nose."

Dog felt herself go cold.

"I couldn't possibly sell it," said Uncle. "At least," he added slyly, "not for as little as that."

"No?" said the man. "What's so special about it?"

Dog hated him already. His voice was

cruel, like Uncle's voice but thinner, sharper.

"Just some funny-looking mongrel, innit?"

Dog realized that Uncle was getting cross, but not too cross, because here was a chance to make more money.

"It is a rare *coatimundi*," he said, in his poshest tones, "from" – he hesitated and looked up at his map: he really wasn't sure where Esme was from – "from the forests of Timbuktu!"

"Oh yeah?" said the man. "I'll give you twenty for it then."

Uncle gave a pretend laugh. "Lowest I could consider is a hundred."

The man laughed back nastily. "Thirty, tops," he snapped.

"Seventy-five," Uncle snapped back, and they began to exchange prices as if they were playing ping-pong.

38

"Thirty-five."

"Seventy."

"Forty."

"Sixty."

"Fifty."

"Fifty-five?"

"Done."

Dog couldn't believe it. In less time than it took to feed a hamster, her friend and companion had been sold!

"Good," said the sharp-voiced man. "Have it packed up and ready for tomorrow morning. I'll pick it up as soon as you're open."

Of course, Esme had no idea what had happened. At bedtime Dog let her out of her cage and she curled up happily in Dog's arms, closing her eyes as she popped the ripe grapes in her teeth. She didn't understand why Dog was crying, and she snuffled at the salty tears

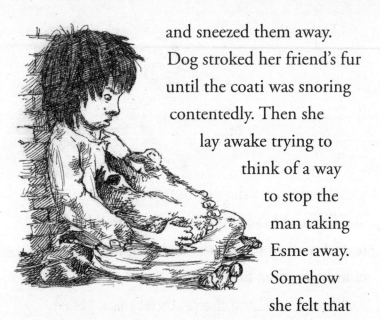

and sneezed them away.
Dog stroked her friend's fur
until the coati was snoring
contentedly. Then she
lay awake trying to
think of a way
to stop the
man taking
Esme away.
Somehow
she felt that
Carlos was trying to think of a way too. He
was whispering from the darkness of his locked
cage, but his voice was so worn out after a day
of mimicking that it was too quiet to hear. At
last Dog fell asleep, her arms around Esme.

But Carlos was awake, rasping to himself
over and over, like the creak of an open door.
"*Escape!*" he said. "*Escape!*"

Chapter 9

Dog didn't want the morning to come, but it did. There was nothing she could do about it. She made a special breakfast for Esme, but Uncle came downstairs early, before she had time to enjoy it, and pushed Esme into her cage. Then, from behind the counter, he pulled out the box, the black, black box, just large enough to hold one old, fat coati. He left it waiting, open and gaping like a mouth, for Esme's new owner to arrive. Dog wondered if she could somehow get into the box with Esme, so at least they would be together – the man couldn't be any worse than Uncle.

But even if she could, what would happen to Carlos?

When Esme saw the box, she began to chitter with fear. Dog sat by her cage, stroking her long nose through the wire and trying to make her feel better, but Uncle dragged her away.

"Get up. Stop your snivelling, you lazy, useless good-for-nothing," he snarled. "Get to *work*! Get that bird sorted *now*! We'll have customers in half an hour!"

Uncle kept the key to Carlos's cage, but Dog was the only person Carlos allowed near. He'd even taken to snapping his beak menacingly at customers who came within a wing's length. So Uncle kept clear as Dog let Carlos out of his cage and took him for his morning poo in the customer toilet. He liked to be left to poo in private and it took ages, which made Uncle very agitated. Did he imagine a bird was going to swim round the U-bend? Dog wondered to herself.

But this morning was different. Carlos was done in no time at all, and called to her softly from inside the WC! "*Dog! Dog!*"

Dog went in to find him clinging to the brickwork, halfway up the end wall.

"*Look!*" he said, sounding very excited. "*Look!*"

Dog looked. All she could see were the usual bare bricks.

She shrugged at the parrot.

"*Watch!*" Carlos hissed, then pulled a bit of mortar out from between two bricks with his strong curved beak and, with a deft little flick, threw it into the toilet.

"*Whoosh! All gone,*" he said gleefully.

Dog looked at the bricks more closely. The mortar that held them in place was missing from an area about the size of a small door. One push, and that bit of wall would collapse. Dog was astonished. This was what Carlos had been doing every morning, not huge poos at all!

"*Escape!*" whispered the bird. "*Escape!*"

Dog wished that Esme was with her now, this minute, and that they could crash through the wall and get away together. But Esme was in her cage and Uncle was banging angrily on the WC door.

"Get that bird out here, you useless
mongrel," he shouted.

The parrot flapped calmly onto Dog's
shoulder. "*Escape*," he said again, very quietly,
"*later!*"

Dog's heart beat wildly, with fear and
excitement. If Esme was going to "escape" too,
then there wasn't very much "later" left.

Chapter 10

By the time the man with the sharp voice arrived, the shop was full of visitors. A class of school children and their teachers were standing around "Polly", and Uncle was trying to sell them nasty cheap sweets and fizzy drinks. The man had to speak quite loudly to make himself heard over the squeals and giggles of the children.

"I said I wanted it all packed up and ready!" He sounded even sharper than before.

"I'm just about to do it!" said Uncle. "Just had a few little delays this morning."

The truth was, Uncle was rather afraid

that Esme would bite him, now that she understood what was happening.

"Hurry up!" said the man. "I haven't got all day!"

Dog trembled behind the door of the storeroom. In a moment it would be too late, and Esme would be gone for ever. She didn't know what she was going to do, but she had to do something. If Esme was gone, then it wouldn't matter if she too was taken in a black, black box; it wouldn't matter what Uncle did to her.

So Dog stepped out of the storeroom and into the shop, where the visitors could see her.

Everything went quiet as all eyes turned to look at her. Dog had no idea how she appeared to other people: a tiny, barefoot, starved-looking child, obviously bruised and battered, and dressed in an old sack, with hair and skin that had never been washed.

The sharp man, who was very clean and
fastidiously neat, was shocked. "*What is that?*"
he said, stepping back towards the door and
clutching his wad of notes close to his chest.

Uncle laughed nervously, and began to go very, very red. "Get back in the storeroom, there's a good Dog!" he said, trying to sound nice and managing to sound nastier than ever.

Dog was terrified by the sight of so many staring faces, and by the horrible, familiar threat in Uncle's voice. But she wasn't going to turn back now. She thought of the wall, just waiting to be broken, and shook her head.

Uncle was turning almost purple with rage. "Dog, I told you to get back!"

Again, Dog shook her head. With her hands shaking and her knees knocking, she went to Esme's cage and opened the door. In a second Esme was wrapped around her shoulders, hugging her like a live shawl.

"You call your child *Dog*?" asked the bossiest-looking teacher.

"No, no, no," said Uncle, trying to fake a

laugh but sounding as if he was choking. "Just a nickname . . ." he blustered. "She's nothing to do with me anyway. She's a deaf-mute, poor little thing. Lives next door. Nothing to do with me, really—"

But Uncle's voice interrupted the real Uncle.

"*Dog, Dog!*" said the parrot, in perfect imitation of the horrible way Uncle had spoken to Dog every day of her life. "*Get out here!*" The voice was so full of cruelty and malice that all the children and teachers gasped in horror.

"*Stop your snivelling,*" snarled Uncle's voice, "*you lazy, useless, good-for-nothing mongrel. Get to work!*" Then Carlos imitated the unmistakable sound of a slap.

Everyone looked from the parrot to Uncle. They all knew that the parrot was the most honest of witnesses; a bird, after all, couldn't really *speak*, only repeat exactly what it had heard. Hadn't they all been watching it do just that before this little waif had appeared in the room?

Carlos snipped through the leather thongs that tied his feet to the perch, and in two flaps was sitting on Dog's outstretched arm. All the while he kept on talking in Uncle's voice, saying all the things that Uncle had said behind the closed doors of the pet shop.

"*And you'd better hide in that storeroom,*" Carlos said, "*because if anyone — anyone at all — sees you, you'll be taken away in a black, black box and that will be the end of you!*"

Some of the younger children began to cry.

Uncle's words fell all around him like bars as, stony-faced and silent, the children, the teachers and even the pointy, sharp-voiced man, closed in on him.

"*Now!*" rasped the parrot in its own voice.

Dog knew just what to do. With Esme holding on tight and Carlos flapping behind her, she sped through the door she knew said CUSTOMER WC on it and leaned on the weakened wall with all her might. The bricks collapsed with a crash as Dog, Esme and Carlos rushed out into the wide world.

Chapter 11

Esme and Dog clung to each other; it was
wonderful to be free, but scary too. Above
the high brick walls behind the shop, the sky
showed wide and blue. The sight of all that
space and light made Dog feel giddy; she
wanted to gaze up at it, but there was no
time to stop. Loud voices were calling
from the broken wall, and running footsteps
began to follow them. Dog ran with Esme
perched on her shoulder, following the
parrot as he flew ahead of them, twisting and
turning down a maze of alleyways. He
didn't hesitate for a moment and seemed

to know his way as well as he knew his own feathers.

The voices and footsteps faded into the distance far behind them, but Dog felt certain

that Uncle would search for them, so she
was glad that the bird kept flying. On and
on, between high walls, behind tall buildings
and rows of little houses, down empty streets
lined with rubble. Dog glimpsed bare winter
gardens; lines of washing; prams and sheds
and dustbins; a world of life she'd never seen
before. Once, a flock of small dark birds passed
low overhead; Dog heard the thrilling rush of
their wings and her heart sang.

At last Carlos stopped flying, and came to
rest on Dog's shoulder. "*Here!*" he said, but
"here" didn't feel like much of a destination.

They stood at the bottom of a narrow
dead-end street clogged with bulging bin bags;
rusting supermarket trolleys toppled in a small
sea of oily puddles. In front of them was the
wall of a huge warehouse, and in that wall,
one tiny corrugated-iron door with a little

yellow knob. There were all sorts of noises coming through the wall – voices, bangs, crashes and shouts. Dog was frightened. Where there were people, there might be Uncle out to catch her. But Carlos made the sound of a creaky door opening and it was clear he wanted them to go inside. Dog turned the knob and the door opened with just the same sound as the parrot had made.

Chapter 12

Inside the warehouse was a market, with stalls stretching out for as far as Dog could see – hundreds of them, selling every kind of fruit and vegetable. Dog, with Esme and Carlos perched on her shoulders, stepped through the narrow doorway and found herself at the shadowy back of one of these stalls, much to the surprise of the lady stallholder, who almost fell off her chair.

"*Eady!*" said Carlos loudly. "*Eady!*" And fluttered his wings at her.

"Oh my Lord!" said the lady, and her round face got even rounder. "We haven't seen you in a long time!" For a moment Dog was confused: nobody apart from Uncle and the people in the shop had ever seen her; then she realized that this Eady woman was talking to Carlos.

"George, George!" Eady called to the man packing oranges into a box at the front of the stall. "Look who's come to see us!"

George, who was tall as well as round, ducked under the awning and broke into a huge grin at the sight of the parrot. "Well, I'll be—"

Before George had the chance to say any more, Carlos had flown onto his shoulder, squawking and flapping excitedly, exclaiming, "*George, George, George!*"

George reached up and scratched the bird on the back of his neck, just the way Dog did. Dog felt a little hurt that Carlos was greeting these strangers so warmly.

"I'm sure we're very glad to see you too, Carlos, old boy," George laughed. "Very glad indeed."

Dog hung back, uncertain how to behave and afraid that she and Esme would be forgotten now that Carlos was with his old friends. She buried her nose in Esme's fur and wished they could just go somewhere on their own.

But George and Eady were far too hospitable to ignore any guest in their stall.

"I think you'd better introduce us to your new mates, Carlos!" said George.

The parrot shuffled down George's arm and hopped deftly onto the back of Eady's chair. He inclined his head first to Esme, then to Dog. "*Esme,*" he said, and then, "*Dog.*"

"Dog?" said Eady and George together, and Carlos spoke in Uncle's voice:

"Lazy, good-for-nothing Dog!"

Hearing Uncle's voice, Esme put a paw over her eyes, and Dog shuddered. George and Eady exchanged a long look and a nod.

"Right!" said George, bending down to speak quietly to Dog. "We get the picture, love. Carlos is good at givin' the picture, i'n't you, boy?"

Eady looked carefully into Dog's worried face. "Don't you fret," she said. "You're safe as houses here. We'll shut the stall up directly, then we'll have something to eat, eh? Your little mate there looks like she might be partial to grapes."

Esme took her paw away from her eyes and wiffled her nose hopefully in Eady's direction; Esme didn't have much of a vocabulary but she knew what "grapes" meant.

Dog huddled on a stool near the door, with

Esme popping grapes on the floor beneath her, while Eady and George pulled down the shutters. Soon they were enclosed in a cosy little world of fruit and veg, singing kettles and rattling tin cups. Dog had no idea how to behave with humans. Even being looked at was strange and rather uncomfortable at first. She took food when it was offered to her, hardly daring to look up, but George and Eady didn't seem to mind. They chatted to each other as if Dog, Esme and Carlos were the sort of guests they entertained every day of the week.

While Dog ate her tenth slice of bread and butter (something she'd never eaten before and was finding particularly delicious), Eady fussed around her with clothes pulled from an old case at the back of the shop.

"Here we are," she said with satisfaction.

"That's what you need to keep the cold out, my girl."

Dog knew about doing what she was told, so she let Eady manoeuvre her into a pair of trousers and a jersey. Both were far too big, but Eady soon had the sleeves and legs of both garments neatly rolled up to fit.

"Wish I had something better than this for your little tootsies," she said as she helped Dog into a pair of red wellies.

Dog had never worn anything but an old sack before,

so her new outfit felt strange. She liked the trousers and the jersey – they were both soft and fluffy inside; it was as if she had fur like Esme, she thought happily. But she wasn't sure about the wellies. It was hard to move if you couldn't feel the ground. Dog shuffled back to her stool by the door, and pulled her knees up to her chin.

George wrapped his big hands around a third mug of hot sweet tea and gave a deep sigh. "What are your plans then?" he asked.

There seemed to be a lull in the conversation. Eady poured tea, Esme munched more grapes and Carlos cracked another Brazil nut. George asked his question again, and Dog suddenly realized that he was looking at her. She peeped up at him from under the dark mat of her fringe. George's eyes were resting on her, light and warm, the way sunlight used to rest on her skin, shining like a blessing through the old pet-shop window. Never before had Dog been asked a question that she wanted to reply to. She felt in her throat for her voice, like someone reaching into a dark cupboard that has been shut for a long time. But she couldn't find it.

Carlos swallowed a piece of nut and spoke up for her. "*Home,*" he said.

"Home?" said George and Eady together.

Carlos flapped from the back of a chair to land on Dog's shoulder. He tidied up a stray bit of her hair with his beak, then said again, more firmly, "*Home.*"

"Which home, Carlos?" asked George quietly. "You've had few of those over the years. And which of them would do for your new friends?"

George is right, you know," Eady chipped in, wagging her finger at the parrot now. "Which of your old homes would do for a little girl like Dog here? Doctor Alavarez? Mad as a hatter, and dead this long while besides. Madame Boursini's? You couldn't stand all that crystal-ball and Ouija-board nonsense yourself. What d'you think a child would make of it? And as for Miss Waspie! Well, you know perfectly well she isn't a trapeze artist. You can't take a child to any of those places."

Eady rolled her eyes in disapproval, but Dog was fascinated; she had no idea what a hatter was, or a Ouija board or a trapeze artist, but they sounded exciting. What a life this bird had lived!

"Seems to me," said George, "that you've got responsibilities now."

Carlos ruffled his feathers so they stood

out like a pile of raked leaves and brushed Dog's cheek. He shut his eyes. There was a moment of awkward silence, then Carlos's eyes snapped open and his feathers grew sleek; Eady and George smiled at each other and then at Carlos.

"You've got an idea, haven't you, you crafty bird?" Eady laughed.

Carlos tipped his head to one side. "*Marmalade*," he said. "*Old Marmalade*."

"Well," said George, "that's going back a few years."

"Do you still know where to find her, Carlos?" Eady asked.

But Carlos had no time to answer, because there was a sudden loud hammering on the closed metal blinds at the front of the stall.

"Open up, open up. Police!"

Dog leaped to her feet, sure that Uncle himself was outside waiting to catch her. In a second, Esme was in her arms, and Carlos flapping at the door, calling, "*Out! Out! Out!*"

George and Eady exchanged one of their deep looks.

"No time to get to the bottom of this, is there?" Eady said.

"No," said George, and reached for the lock. "Take care of yourself, Carlos. I know you'll take care of your friends. Don't forget we're always here to help!"

George pushed the door open, and the three companions rushed out into the frosty air.

Chapter 13

The street on the other side of the little iron door was empty, but Dog heard the wail of sirens arching over the top of the warehouse, like Uncle's fingers reaching out to grab her. She ran, a little awkward in her new wellies, dodging the bin bags and trolleys, while Carlos flew on ahead. She fixed her eyes on him and tried to push away the feeling that Uncle was waiting at every corner with the black, black box in his hand, its lid gaping wide to swallow them all.

Once again Carlos flew down the quietest back streets. There were few people, and the only cars seemed to be parked; the three companions ducked behind them, trying to creep unnoticed past the old ladies and pram-pushing dads that they met.

Dog had never run so much in all her life. Just when she thought she couldn't keep going for another second, Carlos stopped and landed on some tall iron railings.

He looked around, as if reminding himself of something, then rasped one word at Dog – "*Wait!*" – before flapping off over the railings into the garden beyond, where Dog and Esme could not follow.

For a moment Dog was too out of breath to worry about where Carlos had gone. She sank down, her chest still heaving, and peeled Esme from her aching shoulders.

They were in a wide road with rather grand houses on either side. Cars whizzed by in the distance where their road ran into another, but otherwise it was quiet, which meant they had outrun the sirens.

Dog got her breath back but still Carlos did not return. Every second he stayed away seemed longer and longer, and Dog grew anxious.

Then a large blue car with black windows pulled round the bend in the road and came towards them. To Dog's horror, it slowed, then stopped right beside them. Dog was rooted to the spot with fear, sure that Uncle was about to climb out of it.

If she could scream now, Dog thought, Carlos would come and save them, but her throat was tight and dry with silence.

With a sinister, expensive buzz, the driver's window slid down and a face looked out of the car. It wasn't Uncle! It was a woman with shiny, whipped-up hair, her mouth pink as a mouse's nose. Her eyelids were green like a lizard's and her tongue darted slyly from between her teeth.

"You're that child, aren't you?" she said. "The one from the pet shop? It was all over the lunch-time news."

The woman smiled a dazzling kind of smile,

but her eyes looked at Dog just as a lizard looks at crickets the moment before it eats them. "I think," she said, still smiling like a reptile, "you should come with me!"

Dog held Esme close and wondered how far she could run before Lizard Woman would catch them.

"*Hhhhherrrr!*" The most horrible wheezing noise came from the railings behind her. "*Hhhhherrrr! Hhhhherrrr!*" The sound was very loud and close now; Dog didn't dare look round and see what was causing it. She felt caught between the wheezing and the smile, like a flea between two teeth.

There was a screeching sound of very unhappy metal, and a gate opened in the railings right beside Dog and Esme. Through it came a tall, orange gas canister on rickety wheels, with Carlos perched, wobbling slightly, on top. A small, very ancient lady in a green velvet coat was pushing the gas bottle, to which she was connected by a long tube that ran from it into each of her nostrils. She was as wrinkled as crumpled newspaper, with hair as orange as the canister, standing up from her head like a flame-coloured exclamation mark.

"*Hhhhhherrrrrr!*" she wheezed, breathing through the long tube to her nose. When she'd taken a truly enormous breath, she spoke to Lizard Woman.

"Juliette," she said in a quiet, raspy voice, "these are guests of mine, so there is no need for you to mention this to anyone, is there?"

Lizard Woman's smile had disappeared, and had been replaced by a vague frown, as if her face had been caught in a fog.

"And it might be rather good," the old lady continued, "if you just had a little snooze in your car, right now."

Her voice was papery and soft; it reminded Dog of dreaming, of being very cosy and falling asleep. It obviously reminded Lizard Woman of the same things because she had dropped her head to her steering wheel and was snoring gently.

"*Hypnotism!*" commented Carlos as he made a short glide to land on Dog's shoulder and gently nibbled on her hair.

"Quite so, Carlos," said the red-headed lady, smiling at the bird. "Still an awfully useful skill."

Carlos flapped his wings and blew Dog's hair about in the draught. "*Marmalade!*" he exclaimed. "*Marmalade!*"

"Of course!" wheezed the red-haired lady. "I haven't introduced myself to your friends. I am Marmalade Zee, an old friend of Carlos. Now let's get inside before my nosy neighbour wakes up."

And with that, and another huge, wheezing gasp, she shuffled back through the gate, with her canister clanking and wobbling beside her, and a small girl, a parrot and a coati following behind.

Chapter 14

Marmalade Zee's house stood at the end of
the long, tangled garden. Dog saw that it had
once been beautiful: tall and elegant, with
big windows and balconies, a steep, pointy
roof and chimneys reaching proudly up into
the sky, high above other, more ordinary,
houses. But now it looked rather like its owner,
crumpled and creased, as if it was just too
much effort to stand up and keep all its floors
and windows in straight lines. Many of the
panes were broken, and one of the chimneys
had fallen and made a big hole in the roof.
Climbing plants had completely overgrown

the doors and windows on the ground floor, so Marmalade led them, wheezing, along a sloping path that wound up to a terrace, level with the first floor. She pushed open a glass door with her stick and held aside a curtain to let them in: warm yellow light shone out into the blue-grey winter dusk, and Dog felt that, in spite of all its broken glass and crumbling walls, the house was still cheerful and ready to offer welcome.

They stepped into a huge room lit by a number of hissing gas lanterns standing on the floor, and the last of the day's light, gleaming faintly through huge windows that reached almost up to the high ceiling and down to the floor. The room was crowded with furniture, piled up in layers and towers and stacks, as if all the chairs and tables and beds and chests of drawers in the whole house had come into this one room for refuge. The only useable space was around a tent, pitched in the middle of the room. Beside the tent was a long sofa, and in front of it a fat-bellied stove whose wonky metal chimney disappeared through the ceiling between several enormous crystal chandeliers.

Marmalade waved a vague hand at the tent as she sank down onto the sofa. "Awful hole in the roof, but the tent keeps the water off!"

Dog didn't need the explanation; she had never seen the inside of a normal house, and didn't know that people don't usually camp indoors.

She noticed that Marmalade had organized her room very cleverly, so that she could do most of what she needed to while sitting on the sofa: on one side of the stove, a bucket caught drips from a hole in the ceiling, and on the other, bits of broken furniture were piled in a large basket to fuel to fire. Marmalade had only to lean forward a little, as she was doing now, to put more wood on the fire (a fat section of table leg, carved in a spiral) and scoop water from the bucket into a kettle, which she plonked on the stove.

"There now," she said brightly. "Tea in five minutes."

Marmalade pulled a large biscuit tin out from behind the cushions. The smell of coconut macaroons drew Esme like a magnet. In a moment she had joined Marmalade and Carlos on the sofa and was munching happily. But Dog hung back, not sure how to fit in with another of Carlos's old friends.

"Please," Marmalade said to her, "come and sit with us. Any friend of Carlos is a friend of mine. Carlos and I have known each other for a very long time."

"*A very long time!*" agreed Carlos.

Marmalade delved into the cushions behind her and pulled out a framed picture. "Look," she said, holding the picture for Carlos to see. "Do you remember this?"

Carlos peered at it, first with one eye and then the other, flapped his wings and squawked, "*Carlos!*" he exclaimed. "*Baby Carlos!*"

Dog's curiosity overcame her shyness. She climbed onto the sofa, accepted a biscuit and leaned in to look at the photograph that Marmalade held.

It was very sunny in the photograph, and very, very green, with lots of big plants and leaves all around the four people who stood looking out. Three of the people didn't have many clothes on. They had thick fringes of dark hair and big smiles. One of them was a woman, one was a man and one was a child. The man held a pointed stick and wore some beads around his neck, and the woman had a pattern of red paint on her forehead.

Looking at these people made Dog's heart race; she had never seen them before and yet something about them was familiar.

Between the man and the woman stood Marmalade, looking much less crumpled and creased, and with no orange gas bottle or tubes up her nose. Her red hair was long and shiny and caught up in a fat plait over one shoulder. She held her hands out like a cup, and in the cup was a parrot chick, with a big wobbly-looking head and a few tufts of feathers showing like dots of paint on its pink skin.

"It was taken a very long time ago,"

Marmalade told Dog. "More than thirty years now. I was working in the Amazon, in South America, studying a tribe there, the Maohuri. Well, that's what I said I was doing. Really I was a bit like you – running away!" Her laugh changed into a fit of wheezing and it was a few moments before she could speak again.

"I lived in a great forest by a river, with this family," Marmalade continued, pointing a knobbly finger at the three people in the picture. "That's Dawa and her daughter, Mankamo, and that's Gikita – he was a fine hunter. And this," she said, tapping the parrot chick, "is Carlos. Gikita climbed a tree to take him from a nest and gave him to me."

Dog looked in awe at Carlos: he really was very, very old indeed!

"I didn't want to take a parrot from its

wild home," Marmalade went on, "but the Maohuri kept lots of different animals – birds, coatis – and it would have been rude to refuse Gikita's gift. Anyway, we were friends from the start!"

Carlos squawked again and flapped in agreement.

"We lived like parrots and coatis, all together under the trees."

Marmalade's face shone with this memory. Dog's face was shining too. She didn't know what tribes were, or Theamazun, or Sufmerika, but now she knew what Carlos meant when he said "home". It was the place where he was hatched, a real place where parrots and coatis and people all lived together, free and happy. Dog's heart did somersaults.

Marmalade took some more gasping breaths, and managed to say, "I would be living there still, but I got sick and I had to come back here. I never saw Dawa or Mankamo or Gikita again."

"*Carlos!*" Carlos said, and Marmalade smiled.

"Yes, yes, I had you, Carlos – for a while at least!"

Carlos fluffed out his feathers and pulled his head into his neck.

"Yes, you remember, don't you?" said Marmalade. "Flying off out of that window? I was so worried."

"*Came back!*" Carlos rasped sulkily.

"Yes, you did after *three years!*" Marmalade waggled her finger at him and he caught it playfully in his beak.

She laughed. "You old rogue!" she said.

The kettle on the stove began to whistle. Marmalade pulled a teapot, cups and more biscuits from under the sofa and behind cushions.

When the tea was made, Dog sipped, and dunked chocolate fingers, with all she had heard whirling around her head. She looked at Carlos in wonder. He really was *ancient*. But parrots lived a long time, so he wouldn't die soon.

"I'm very glad to see you, old friend," Marmalade was telling Carlos, "but I have the feeling you are not here to stay, are you?" She raised an enquiring eyebrow at Carlos.

"*Home,*" he said. "*Home!*"

"Yes." Marmalade nodded. "I guessed that's what you'd want. And you'll take your friends of course. I haven't seen a coati or a child like this since I left the Amazon."

Carlos climbed onto her shoulder and looked carefully into her face. "*Marmalade come too?*" he said.

Marmalade's eyes glittered with tears. "I'm too sick, Carlos. But I'm happy that you are going back at last."

For a moment they sat in silence while Marmalade took several long breaths. Then she got to her feet.

"We must be practical," she said. "You can't go in an ordinary way. You will have to stow away on a boat. Luckily, just the right one is in port right now. Come and see."

Marmalade pushed her gas bottle across to one of the tall windows, and Dog and Esme followed sleepily. It had grown dark outside. Dog looked out in wonder at the jumble of streetlights in the blackness.

Although Dog never knew it, the city

where she had lived almost all her life was a
great port, with huge cargo ships from all over
the world coming
and going to and
from the docks.
From Marmalade's
windows they could
see the ships lined
up ready for their
cargos; the cranes;
and dockworkers
running about
like ants under the
floodlights; the dark
sea and sky beyond.
Dog didn't really
understand what
they were looking at.
   But Carlos did.

Marmalade looked through binoculars and pointed out the smallest ship moored at the dock, still huge but not the monster size of the others. "That's the one," she said. "The *Marilyn*. She crosses the Atlantic, then trades along the stretch of coast where your home-river has its mouth."

"*Marilyn*," said Carlos thoughtfully. "*Marilyn*."

"She's loading now," Marmalade told him, "so she'll sail tonight."

Smoke puffed from the *Marilyn*'s chimney and her horn blew low and deep, signalling her readiness to depart.

"No time for goodbyes now, Carlos," wheezed Marmalade. "You must hurry!"

Chapter 15

They left quietly, slipping down the side of
Marmalade's great crumbling house and into
the front garden, as overgrown as the back had
been. None of the streetlights worked, so the
road outside was too dark for Carlos to fly.
He perched on Dog's arm and directed her,
confidently telling her left, right or straight.
His voice was quiet but he seemed to know
what to do, and Dog was happy to follow.

She felt hopeful. Her head felt like a clean
drinking bowl, washed out and clear, not full
of confusing mucky bits. They were going to
get on a big boat – that's what stowing away

was – and they would be a very long way away from Uncle and the black, black box. They were going to the place that had been Carlos's home, and live under a tree.

But getting on the boat would be difficult and dangerous. She would have to concentrate hard. So she pushed away the wondering that was deeper inside – about the people in the photograph and whether she too had been hatched in a forest by a river and somehow been stolen away.

Carlos's directions seemed to be leading them towards more noise and bustle and light. Dog tried to keep calm but she grew very anxious. Every footstep, every voice could be Uncle ready and waiting; every car could be carrying him closer to them.

They wound their way down steep roads and back alleys, and then into wide cobbled streets between tall stone buildings. The air smelled different here. It reminded Dog of the cuttlefish bones she sometimes gave the budgies, and the weed that grew in the goldfish tanks.

The three friends scuttled along in the shadows, running from one darkened doorway to the next. At the end of the cobbled streets, the shadows ran out. The stone and concrete became sea, and the side of the *Marilyn* stretched up into the dark and mist of the night. Piles of huge crates and boxes stood on the dock beside it, moved about by forklift

trucks and cranes; powerful lamps sliced the
night into stripes of shadow and brightness.
Men shouted and vehicles beeped. It looked
like a total muddle.

Just as Dog was taking in this scene, the
sirens that she had thought they had escaped
hours ago began again. Police cars screeched to
a stop in the street where they were hiding, and
policemen began probing the dark doorways
with torches, dogs and shouting.

They flattened themselves against the wall. They were trapped between the busy dock and the police, who were getting closer and closer. Carlos was silent. Dog could feel him hesitating. Her heart raced faster and faster as the voices of the police and the barking of their dogs came nearer. She couldn't stand it for another moment.

Without waiting for Carlos's instructions, she ran, darting in amongst the chaos of the cranes and crates and busy men, using all the tricks she'd learned from years of staying invisible.

Just as the police cars arrived on the dockside, Dog found a slit in a large empty crate, and with Carlos clutched in her arms

and Esme on her shoulder, she slipped inside.
They crouched in the darkest corner and
waited.

"*Good!*" whispered Carlos. "*Clever! Very!*"

Outside, a man with a headlamp and a
bright orange waistcoat shouted up to the
crane driver, telling him which crate to grab
in the machine's jaws. "This one next, Steve.
Ready? Up!" His voice was so loud that it
sounded above the clatter and shouting all
around. Each time he slapped a crate, it was

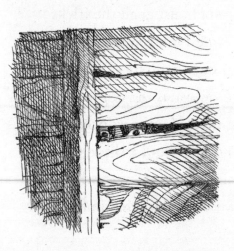 scooped
up and
disappeared
into the
dark body
of the ship.

Peeping
back through

the slit in the crate, Dog could see the
policemen moving amongst the dockers,
getting closer and closer. At last one officer was
standing right by their crate, talking to Orange
Waistcoat Man. Dog could have reached
through the slit and knocked his helmet off
with her hand. Orange Waistcoat Man cupped
his ear to try and hear what the policeman
was saying, but it was too noisy, so he led the
policeman away, to find somewhere quiet. Dog
realized she had been holding her breath. She
let it out shakily.

Carlos spoke. "*Phew*," he whispered. "*Very*."

Esme hid her nose in the straw in the corner
of the crate, but Dog and Carlos peered out
again. The police were starting to look inside
the crates – poking their big torches through
the slats and shining the beam around! Their
only chance now was if their crate was loaded

before the policemen arrived.

Dog guessed what Carlos would do just in time to get her fingers in her ears.

"*HUUUUP! This one next, Steve. Ready? Up!*" he shouted through the slit. He was certainly as loud as Orange Waistcoat Man, and even managed to copy the sound of the man's big flat hand slapping the wooden side of the crate.

At once, the crane's claws fixed on them, and up they went, so fast that Dog felt as if her stomach had been left somewhere much closer to the ground. For a moment the dock, crisscrossed with lights and dotted with policemen, was laid out below them like a toy. Then they were swooping down onto the deck of the boat, bumping onto a forklift truck and swirling down a long ramp into the hold. Esme and Carlos, their claws like hooks, managed to cling to the sides, but Dog rolled around like a peanut in a jar.

At last they were set down. Dog picked herself up, feeling bruised and giddy, and peered around in the gloom. They had got away from the police, but in the corner of the crate, with wild staring eyes and the biggest, shiniest knife Dog had ever seen, was a fourth stowaway.

Chapter 16

The man was huge. Much taller than Uncle, and wider too, though not at all soft and wobbly like Uncle was. In fact, where the light fell on him through the holes in the crate, he looked hard as marble. His eyes were wide, with so much white showing that the dark circle in the middle looked like a little hole. He stood with his feet apart and the knife held blade up in front of him.

"One word," breathed the man. "One single sound . . ." His voice was quiet and dry, like the scuttle of scorpion or a snake's slither. "One single sound, one little move, and . . ." He turned the knife slowly to show its sharp, sharp edge and let it speak his threat for him.

"I didn't give all those policemen out there the slip just for you to give me away. Don't move. Don't even breathe. Maybe I'll mince you anyway, to be sure," he whispered.

Dog thought she could see right through his hard shiny face to the meaning of his words. She imagined herself and her friends as a neatly minced pile of flesh and fur and feathers. So was this man who the sirens had been sounding for? Not for her and Esme and Carlos? She couldn't be sure. One step outside the crate could still mean they would be sent straight back to Uncle. It was better to take their chances where they were.

Outside in the hold, voices shouted instructions and the little trucks zoomed about as the last of the cargo was loaded. Inside the crate the seconds crawled by. The man went on staring, holding up his blade like a horrible promise, and the three friends went on being rooted to the spot in double fear: of being discovered and of being minced to bits.

Just as Dog was deciding that she couldn't stand another slow second of thinking of herself and her friends being shredded, the noise in the hold died down. The men and their trucks were gone, and the heavy door above them creaked and scraped as it slid shut. Everything was suddenly quiet and, even more suddenly, totally dark.

In half the time it takes for a heart to beat, time went from crawl to sprint, so that several things seemed to happen all at once. The man made a kind of snarling noise and lurched forward, his heavy tread making the boards underfoot creak and grumble. Dog threw herself back, away from the whoosh of the knife slicing through the space where she had just stood. She fell against the wall behind her and scrabbled with her arms spread wide to try and feel for the touch of fur or feather.

Her left hand closed on Esme's nose, and her right was seized by the familiar horny clawed foot of the parrot. A moment later they were all tumbling backwards through the slit in the crate in a tangle of tails and wings and arms.

The man's wheezing voice followed them, not quite forming words any more, but howling like an animal in pain. In a panic to escape, Dog crashed into crates and boxes, sacks and packages. Carlos screeched, Esme yelped. Dog fell onto her hands and knees, and squirmed and wriggled between the cargo piled all around, with her friends clinging uncomfortably to her back. Only when she'd crawled down what felt like a mile of gaps, too narrow for any adult to follow, did she feel it was safe to stop and catch her breath.

"*Listen!*" croaked Carlos. "*Listen!*"

She expected to hear that horrible howl again, but instead there was a deep rumbling hum that was spreading through the vessel. It made Dog think of a giant heart, thrub-thrub-thrubbing; she could feel the whole ship waking up and coming alive; her rivets creaked like joints and the water slapped on her metal flanks.

On the decks high above them, huge ropes were cast off, and with a grating growl the great iron anchor was hauled up and put away. Dog felt the ship begin to pitch and roll. This was floating – like the pets' water dishes in the sink, but much, much bigger. She remembered Uncle's "educayshun" again – "the blue part's the sea". The blue part, Dog remembered, went all around the green part – the land – so once you were on it, you could go anywhere; anywhere at all.

"*Home!*" whispered Carlos. "*Going home!*"

But Dog knew that the blue was very big and she suddenly felt very afraid. How would they find the green bit again, let alone a tree to live under? She took a deep breath. Wherever and whatever they did find, at least it wouldn't be any sort of pet shop.

Chapter 17

They rested for a while, leaning against rough sacks stuffed with something hard and lumpy that smelled of oil, huddling close together so as not to lose each other in the blackness. Dog could hear Carlos's feathers ruffle as he put his head under his wing – darkness was like an off-switch for parrots – and Esme snuggled into her lap and began to snore. But Dog stayed awake, still listening for the footsteps of the knifeman, even though she knew the spaces they had crawled through were too narrow for him to follow.

Dog thought again about the map and

the blue sea marked on it. She guessed it was much, much bigger than anything she could imagine. So they could be stuck here with no light, or food or water, for a long time. Animals could live for a while without food or light but not long without water, and already Dog could feel the dryness at the back of her throat. She wondered if you could drink the sea and how you would get to it through this giant metal drinking bowl of a boat.

They couldn't stay where they were, but which way would lead them to a better place? Carlos knew his way around the city, but he didn't know this ship, and anyway, it was dark. As Dog was trying to think what to do, she began to notice small sounds through the hum of the ship's engines: tiny patterings and faint scratchings. She knew what they were at once: rats!

Dog had had many rat friends in the pet shop, and the thought that there were rats – many rats, by the sound of things – on the ship made the darkness seem less frightening. What were they doing here? Had they escaped from a pet shop too?

Dog had an idea: rats were always good at finding food and water, so perhaps the rat sounds might lead them to a better place! She nudged Esme and Carlos awake and, with the two sleepy creatures riding on her back, began to crawl through the gaps between the piles of cargo, following the little scratchings and squeakings. Wherever the gap widened or split in two, Dog listened hard and chose the direction in which the rat sounds were loudest.

She wondered how long they had been crawling in the dark. Was it still night outside or had day come again? Her eyes played tricks on her; coloured dots and blobs swam in front of her. Then they reached a metal wall. Dog turned along it, feeling its surface with her hand, and after a short distance felt the square edge of a door. She stood up. The door didn't have a knob or a handle but it did have a wheel in the middle. Dog turned it one way and then the other until it began to shift. With a kind of clunk and a groan the door swung open just a crack.

On the other side of the door was light, dim and green but definitely light.

Carlos hopped down from Dog's back with a squawk, and one after another the three friends squeezed through the door. They found themselves in an old kitchen, with a cooker that had clearly not been used for years and a dirty rusting sink. Dog turned the taps but nothing came out.

One faint and very dirty light bulb stuck out from the wall above the sink. It gave just enough light to make out stacks of huge tins, each one twenty times the size of a normal cat-food tin, piled on the floor.

It was clear that the tins had been here for a long time: many were rusted and covered in dents, and almost all had lost any sort of label. They smelled rather oily, and Dog doubted if they contained anything that could be eaten or drunk, but then Carlos made an unmistakable slurping noise, like someone sucking the last

bit of milkshake from the bottom of a glass.
Dog and Esme came running.

Carlos had found a tin with the remains of
a label. It showed something that could have
been an orange or maybe a peach – something
edible at any rate.

Carlos half flapped, half climbed up the tin

and, using his beak like a can opener, pierced a hole in the top. Esme and Dog pushed the tin over and a dribble of sticky liquid spilled out onto the floor. Esme licked it up immediately. Carlos made for the next puddle, scooping it up with his beak and then working his tongue to swallow it down. Dog went last, sucking straight from the tiny hole Carlos had made. The liquid was sticky and too sweet, but it tasted lovely and stopped her thirst.

There had been no rat noises for a while, but now Dog noticed she could hear them again, coming from the direction of the door. She realized the rats must have followed them into this old kitchen. For some reason that made her feel suddenly uneasy. And then she heard Esme screech with fear.

Chapter 18

Dog raced towards the sound. Behind a pile of tins, Esme was being attacked by rats with spiky brown coats and mean eyes. They were swarming all over her as she bit and thrashed to get them off.

Never in her life had Dog wanted to scream more than at this moment, but as always her throat was empty. Carlos dropped from somewhere above them and dive-bombed the carpet of rats that was starting to flow towards Dog. It was clear what the rats wanted – fresh meat, not dry scraps and tins their teeth couldn't pierce. They were demented rats, driven mad from being trapped down here in the hold of the ship.

Dog picked Esme up and shook her free of rats, then perched her on her shoulders and began to run, with Carlos flapping at her side.

The doorway they had come through was now dark with rats, so there was no escape there. Dog ran in the opposite direction, towards the far end of the dim kitchen. She swept tins off a pile against the wall, down onto the crowding rats, and as she did so found the bottom rungs of a ladder that disappeared up into darkness.

They were on it in a second. Esme, as best climber, went first, then Dog. Carlos flew in wide spirals to make the climb at the same pace as his friends. Fear made them fast, and they were soon high up, in the dim gloom close to the ceiling. Looking up past Esme's ample bottom, Dog could just make out a kind of little round door in the ceiling.

She stopped to catch her breath, then looked back and saw they had left the rats behind! There they were, far below, a dark tide

against the pale
paintwork of the
deck and the silvery
stacks of tins. But as
Dog watched, the
rats swirled around
the ladder and
began to climb it,
spreading upwards
like a stain. Esme
had seen them too.
She gave a little
grunt and tried to
climb faster, but
she was already
tired and soon the
rats were gaining.
Glancing down
between her feet,

Dog could see the shape of their sharp snouts and the dark glitter of their unblinking eyes, just a few rungs behind!

Carlos had settled on the top of the ladder, clinging upside down and calling to them. "*Quick. Quick!*"

Dog pushed Esme higher and higher until they were both crushed side by side at the top of the ladder, with the strange little door just above them, and Carlos half clinging, half hovering on the last rung.

"*Open! Open! Door open!*" he squawked, but it wasn't so simple. The metal wheel at the centre that must be turned to open the door was stuck. Dog used all her strength, and still it wouldn't budge.

Now the rats had reached Dog's feet; she had to hold on with her hands to free her feet for kicking. Carlos squawked and Esme chittered with fear. Another few moments and the wave of rats would be too dense to simply kick away. Dog and Esme would be covered in them, with the choice of being eaten alive or falling to die on the floor below. Dog's head was filled with hotness and confusion; she tried again to turn the door wheel with one hand but it was no good.

And then Esme did something totally extraordinary. She stopped chittering and clinging on with her eyes closed. She turned round, and went head first down the ladder towards the advancing rats. Holding on with her back legs and her curling stripy tail, she began to snarl and scratch. With her fur on end, and her lips drawn back from her teeth, she looked like a different animal, like her fearsome coati ancestors who had scared away jaguars and anacondas from the treetops.

The rats climbing upwards were faced with sharp slashing teeth that snapped limbs and severed heads. There were fast flailing claws too, ripping their paws from the rungs and uprights of the ladder and sending them spinning into thin air. That wasn't all!

Now the parrot had joined in, swooping at them and knocking them off with its wings and grabbing feet. For a few moments the rats held back, weighing the chances

120

of a fresh meal against the odds of a sudden death. It was all the time Dog needed. With both hands free, she wrenched the wheel again; this time it moved, just a little at first, then faster and faster.

Dog pushed, and with one big shove the round metal door clanged up and back. Dog was through it in a moment, pulling Esme up after her. Below them Carlos dive-bombed a few more rats, then swooped up, folding his wings to shoot through the hatch like a missile. Dog slammed the door shut, trapping the rats down below, then sat down breathless on the floor.

"*Phew!*" said Carlos. "*Very very phew!*"

Chapter 19

Dog had never seen a sky full of stars. The pet-shop window was too grimy and the streetlight outside too glaring to see more than a faint dot of light from the very brightest ones. But the open sky above her now was shimmering with an endless sea of them. She gazed up, mesmerized. She didn't know what stars were, but she was lost in their beauty all the same. Esme pointed her nose straight up and blinked her eyes in wonder.

But Carlos wasn't interested in stars. *"Danger, danger!"* he hissed. *"Must hide! Coming person! Now."*

The sound of footsteps ringing on the metal deck finally got Dog and Esme's attention. Just in time, they scrambled up to one of the lifeboats slung above the deck and wriggled, rather noisily, under its cover.

They lay still in the bottom of the lifeboat, listening as the footsteps got closer and closer, then stopped, right beside them.

A voice spoke very sternly. "I know you're in there; I heard you banging about."

The three friends crouched lower.

The corner of the cover was lifted and a

bright torch beam began to search the boat.

"Just come out and show yourself," said the voice, though now it didn't seem quite so stern. "You can't get away, you know!"

The beam caught them like a spotlight. They huddled together, waiting to be seized. Instead, the voice gave a long, low giggle, and someone jumped in with them, propping the torch up like a lantern to light the whole space under the cover.

"Well, am I glad to see you! After all that clanking of hatches I thought I was going to find some villain with a gun."

The owner of the giggle was a lanky boy dressed in a pair of ancient shorts, a T-shirt with a picture of a beer bottle on the front and a grimy yellow oilskin jacket. Dog looked at him from under the cover of her fringe.

"No need to look so scared!" He grinned. "I don't think you're a danger to the safety of the ship, so I won't give you away, don't worry! Just don't let anyone else see you, or we're all in big trouble."

They were safe! Dog had never hugged a human but she wondered if she should start now. Esme caught her relief and her tail went straight up like a flag.

Carlos, who had been sitting dejectedly on the floor, now clambered onto Dog's shoulder. "*Boy fine, very*," he announced.

The boy was delighted. He smiled as if all his features wanted to join in the fun, even his ears – which, Dog noticed, were large and rather nicely mouse-like.

"Well, that's a compliment if ever I heard one!" he said. "Quite right too. I am a *very* fine boy, though I'm not sure there's anyone else on board that would say so! Anthony Steven Kevin Edwards, at your service. Asky for short, apprentice seafarer extraordinaire!"

He sat down on a coil of rope, grinning, and looked keenly at Dog. "So what's your name then?"

Dog shook her head.

"What?" said Asky. "Not going to tell me your name?"

She shook her head again and looked down at her feet, still inside their small red wellies.

Carlos coughed. "*This*," he said, tapping his curved beak gently on Dog's head, "*Dog, this*." Stretching a wing towards the coati, Carlos went on, "*Esme . . . Me, Carlos*."

Asky looked dumbfounded. "Wow! Not just a talking bird, a thinking one too! You know we're bound for South America, don't you?" he said to Carlos.

Carlos squawked approval and said, "*Sí, sí, sí!*"

"Oh, you already speak the lingo then!" said Asky. "Going to see your family in the jungle, Carlos?"

The parrot stretched his wings around his two friends. "*All see family in the jungle*," he said in Asky's voice.

Asky laughed at Carlos's mimicry but Dog wondered if he was being silly or saying something true. She thought about Marmalade's words:

I haven't seen a coati or a child like this since I left Theamazun.

If Theamazun was where they were going, maybe she and Esme were going home too?

Chapter 20

Asky visited most nights, when it was easy to slip about the decks unseen. He told them the *Marilyn* was owned by his Great-uncle Enoch, who always took the smallest, cheapest crew he could.

"They eat chips when they're off duty and watch satellite TV in the mess. Only person who comes down to this deck is me. If you stay quiet, you ought to be all right down here."

He brought them food – fruit and nuts and crackers, hidden under his T-shirt – and blankets to sleep on. Water was the only problem. Big bottles were hard to hide under a shirt, and Asky could never bring enough, so when it rained they collected the water that ran off the cover of the lifeboat.

Sometimes they rolled back the corner of the lifeboat cover, on the seaward side, and breathed the clean sea air. Esme would stand on tiptoe, poking her nose as high as she could, as if searching for the scent of something. If it was still enough, Carlos would fly alongside them in the starlight, then sit and preen every feather, grumbling to himself about "*Salt! Salt!*"

Dog and Asky would watch the waves rolling along the side of the boat or look up at the stars. Asky had lots to say about stars. "They're like the sun, only a long way away. The sun is a star, just really close."

All the patterns the stars made in the sky had names. "There's Orion. He's always easy to find, that old boy. There's his belt. See? No?"

Dog shook her head. Asky took her hand and pointed with it. "There, those three big 'uns. And the big orange one, that's his shoulder, yeah?"

Dog nodded. She could see Orion now, standing tall, with one arm raised above his head.

"They show the way, stars do," Asky said. "That's how the old seafarin' boys used to navigate. None of your satellite navigation in those days, they just followed the stars!"

Dog didn't know what satellite navigation was, but now she knew what stars were. She watched how they moved across the sky in the night and disappeared below the horizon, in the very direction the *Marilyn* was headed.

When it was too cold, or too wet, which it often was, they sat in the torchlight under the lifeboat cover. Asky thought of questions that Dog could answer with a nod, a shake or a shrug. Even though she couldn't speak, Dog felt that she was talking to a human for the first time in her life.

"So, your mum and dad dead then?"

Dog shrugged and thought of Marmalade's picture – of Gikita and Dawa; had people like that been her parents?

"Were you born in the old port?"

Asky meant the city where the pet shop was. She realized that she now knew she hadn't been born there, that there had been something before Uncle and the pet shop. She shook her head.

"I bet you were born somewhere exciting. Like Carlos's jungle, eh?" Asky said.

Dog smiled: perhaps that was true. She nodded her head again.

"Maybe you hatched from an egg? What do you think?"

Carlos coughed and stopped preening. He looked at Dog and Asky with one eye then the other. "*Hatched from an egg!*" he exclaimed, in Asky's voice, adding, "*No! No! No!*" in his own.

He looked so horrified that Asky and Dog burst out laughing.

"*Rude,*" said Carlos, and turned his back on them. "*Very, very.*"

Chapter 21

The weather got warmer and sunnier with every day at sea. It was too risky to lift the cover when it was light, so daytimes in the lifeboat got hot and stuffy. There was nothing to do but try and keep quiet. Esme was happy to sleep and sleep, but Dog and Carlos needed to find ways to kill their boredom.

Carlos invented bird exercises. He hung from the underside of the cover by his feet and flapped his wings. It kept him occupied and made a nice cooling fan system for the boat. Dog lay propped on lifejackets with her eye next to a chink in the cover that allowed

her to look down at the sea. She watched the
waves and wondered why a colour that could
be so many different things was just called
blue. Sometimes she saw sea creatures – and
she'd point at them to get Carlos to tell her
what they were, or mime their shape and
movement to Asky, who seemed to know
everything.

In this way Dog knew she had seen flying
fish.

"Their fins are like wings," Asky told her, "and you only get them in tropical waters. We're nearly there now, you know!"

Dog saw what Asky said were "dolphins" too. Carlos had got quite excited about those and had inspected them carefully with each eye in turn pressed to the gap in the cover. "*Not fish,*" he'd said. "*Air breathe. Clever.*"

Dog wasn't sure if they were clever for breathing air, or for doing amazing acrobatic leaps out of the water. Clever or not, they seemed to be having a lot of fun.

Days and days passed. Dog couldn't tell how many. She'd thought she was getting to know the sea when, one morning, staring out of her usual chink, it looked different. The blues and greens faded, water and sky changed to grey. Wind whistled, and waves like jagged white teeth covered the sea. The whole ship began to roll and tip so it was hard not to slide about the lifeboat.

The skin around Carlos's beak turned from white to green. "*Sick*," he said. "*Very*."

Then Asky risked a visit in daylight and Dog knew that something was very wrong.

"Can't come in, too many crew about," he whispered from beside the lifeboat. "Listen, there's going to be a storm. A really, really bad storm. The *Marilyn*'ll come through, no worries. But it'll be tough."

All the feathers on Carlos's head stood on end. "*Storm*," he repeated quietly, and shivered.

Dog shuddered too; there was fear under Asky's words.

"Pull the cover on as tight as you can," he told them, "then tie everything down, and rope yourselves to the benches. Got that?"

Asky pushed his hand into the lifeboat.

Carlos gently squeezed a finger in his beak and Esme rubbed his palm with her cold nose. Dog put her small hand inside Asky's, and felt her throat ache with silence.

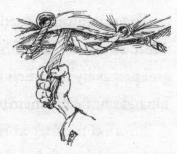

"Take care of yourself, Dog," Asky said, and closed his fingers around hers for a moment. Then he was gone.

Dog, Esme and Carlos worked together to do what Asky had told them. Dog and Esme pulled ropes tight, and Carlos, who was good at knots, tied them off. Then Dog roped herself to one of the benches, and strapped Carlos and Esme safely inside her lifejacket, so they wouldn't all be thrown around like beans in a box. Then they held tight and waited.

First the wind smashed into the ship like a blow from a giant's club. Then the waves grew, until the ship was tossed from peak to trough like a tiny toy. The *Marilyn* screeched and groaned as the sea tried to rip her to pieces, but she held on. The lifeboat rocked and juddered as the wind tried to work it loose. All around, in the weird twilight of the storm, the waves bellowed and the wind shrieked, while the three friends huddled together silently in their little refuge.

The storm went on. It grew dark but there were no stars, only fearsome flashes of terrible brightness, and crashes in the sky. Dog wondered if the sky was breaking and if the stars would fall into the sea.

When the night was at its blackest, and without warning, a terrible howl cut through the screaming wind, and a huge blade ripped

the lifeboat cover in two. Wind and lashing rain burst in on the three terrified friends and a great flash of lightning showed the knifeman towering over them! He was still on the ship, and he had found them!

He was much thinner than when they'd last seen him and his white skin was covered in rat bites, but his great alabaster body still weighted him down in a gale that would have blown Dog away in a second. He rode the bucking, tipping deck as if it were a ballroom floor. His face streamed with rain and his eyes glowed with a feverish excitement. He seemed to be another part of the hurricane.

"You!" he roared. "You! My three first meals you'll be, just as soon as I launch this boat. I've been tormented by police, chewed by rats – I'm not going to drown in this metal coffin."

Then he leaped into the bow of the lifeboat

and began hacking at the ropes that kept
her lashed to the ship! One rope broke, then
another, and then a third.

"*No!*" squawked Carlos. "*Noooooooo!*" He
wriggled free of Dog's lifejacket and took to
the air. The wind blew him straight into the
knifeman's face, where he held on, clawing and
pecking, stopping him from slicing any more
ropes.

But it was too late. As a giant swell struck
the *Marilyn*, it parted the old lifeboat from
her mother-ship as easily as a speck of dust
brushed from a shelf. For a split second they
were all held in the brightness of a lightning
flash – the man falling backwards to be
swallowed by the waves, the bird helplessly
fighting the wind, the girl and coati holding
onto the spinning boat. Then all was darkness
and bellowing sea, as the lifeboat fell down,

down, down into the black trough of a wave.

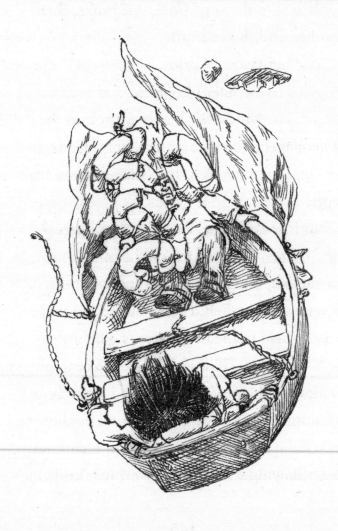

Chapter 22

Dog opened her eyes and saw calm blue sky. The lifeboat was still at last, and it rocked her gently as she lay, comforted by the warmth of the sun. For a moment she was just grateful to be alive, and then she remembered Esme and Carlos, and that terrible fall from the *Marilyn*. Where were her friends? She sat up and looked around with her heart racing.

The storm had carried the lifeboat to land! They floated in a calm, sandy bay, with dense green trees beyond the beach. The air was warm and full of the scent of flowers and plants. Dog thought of the map above Uncle's till, and wondered where they were on it now.

The lifeboat was still in one piece, although almost everything that had been inside it had been stripped away by the wild sea. The ripped cover was knotted around the bow in a complicated tangle. There was a deep puddle in the bottom of the boat, and lying in that,

 like a bit of wet rag, was Esme. Dog tried to get up but found she was still tied to the bench and the knot took minutes to undo. In all that time she didn't see Esme

breathe once.

Free at last, she staggered to Esme's side and gently lifted her out of the water. She hung limply in Dog's arms. Her nose was bloody, her tail was broken and she seemed quite cold. Dog laid her in the driest part of the boat, and gently began to check her friend's little body for signs of life. She cleared the blood from Esme's nose, and put her lips close to the coati's nostrils to feel for breath. Yes! There was the tiniest movement of air and, when she put her hand on Esme's chest, a faint flutter of a heartbeat. She stroked the coati's fur, feeling for any broken bones, and gently massaged her paws to get her circulation moving again. Slowly Esme's breathing deepened, and her heart began to beat more strongly, but still she didn't open her eyes.

Dog felt terribly frightened and alone.

Poor Carlos must be a drowned scrap of blue and gold somewhere in the huge ocean, and Esme's life was hanging by a thread. Even Asky might have gone to the bottom of the sea in the *Marilyn*. She didn't know where she was, or what to do, but she knew she wanted solid land under her feet. She picked up a bit of broken plank, and began to paddle to shore.

The beach was gently sloping and the waves not much more than ripples, so it was easy to get the boat onto the sand. Gently Dog carried Esme up the beach and laid her down in the shade of a palm tree, then went back to the boat to see if there was anything they might find useful. Emergency rations had been washed overboard but the little box marked with a red cross was still in its place. The waves pulled at the boat; soon they might take it out to sea again, and Dog knew she hadn't

148

the strength to haul it far up the beach where the water wouldn't get it. She looked around, trying to think fast. The lifeboat cover, even ripped as it was, might make a good shelter. She tugged at the ropes that Carlos had tied so tightly, and yanked at the cover's edge to free it from the bow. It wouldn't budge, and now the tide was definitely lifting the boat off the sand. She decided to give the cover one more good pull; if it didn't move she'd have to abandon it. She braced her feet and pulled with all the strength she had left. The cover creaked and, with a sound like a wet pancake landing on a kitchen floor, it unravelled itself rather suddenly.

Dog fell backwards, and something was thrown out of the folds and landed with a plop in her lap. It was a large bird, with a hooked beak and sodden ragged feathers.

Carlos coughed mightily, spraying sea water into Dog's face, then opened his eyes. "*Next time*," he said disdainfully, "*aeroplane*."

Chapter 23

Carlos told Dog how to open coconuts by mimicking the sound they made when they were hit with a rock. So they had coconut milk to drink, and sweet white coconut flesh to eat. Esme opened her eyes after the first sip, and was happily munching her way through huge pieces of flesh a day later. They dozed, ate and drank, while their bruises healed and their spirits recovered.

Carlos spent a long time preening. "*Salt!*" he grumbled to himself. "*Salt!*"

Sea water wasn't good for parrot feathers, and for the first day he couldn't fly at all.

Heavy rain early the next morning did the trick. Carlos squawked with such delight as the fresh water soaked his plumage that Dog and Esme came out from the shelter of the trees and shared the shower, the three of them dancing in the downpour together. Then they sat in the sun, dried off, and slept some more!

* * *

When Dog woke again, Carlos was nowhere
to be seen. She wasn't worried – she guessed he
must have missed proper flying; he'd just gone
to stretch his wings.

Esme too was feeling better. Dog had
wrapped
the break in
her tail with
a bandage
from the
lifeboat's
first-aid
kit, and it
showed like a
white flag as
Esme trotted

up and down the beach. She was hunting the
pale blue crabs that scuttled up and down
the beach, batting them with her claws and

reaching down into their narrow little burrows. Dog suddenly felt very, very happy, and she ran off to join Esme on her crab quest.

The crabs danced sideways with a speed that Dog found dazzling. Secretly she thought the crabs far too beautiful to eat, and was quite pleased when Esme dropped her first catch because she didn't expect food to bite back. After that the coati recovered some of her rat-biting fierceness, and the next crab didn't get a chance to nip; Esme crunched it like a boiled sweet the instant she caught it. Dog didn't like that much, but Esme's eating habits were none of her business, and crab hunting was fun. It wasn't until the sun sank behind the treetops that either of them noticed that Carlos hadn't returned.

They sat under their tree and nibbled bits of coconut flesh, scanning the fading sky for

Carlos's silhouette. At last, as the first stars started to prick the blueness, Esme curled her nose into her tail and went to sleep on the warm sand, but Dog didn't feel sleepy at all. She stared out over the whispering sea; this beach was beautiful, but she knew it wasn't the end of their journey.

Chapter 24

Dog fell asleep at last. She dreamed of Carlos flying far away over green treetops, but when she woke in the early morning, he was back. He flapped his wings above her head in great excitement.

"*Home! Home!*" he shouted. "*Get up. Go! Go!*"

Carlos didn't offer any more explanation, and although Esme was reluctant to leave the crabs,

Dog knew it was time to move on. She trusted Carlos to know which direction to take. They bundled up bits of coconut and a medicine bottle of coconut milk in the jersey that Eady had given Dog, and set off along the beach.

They didn't have to walk far. Just a mile or two beyond their beach a river ran muddily into the sea. The far bank was thick with huge trees, but on the nearer bank was a little village of tiny whitewashed houses with tin roofs glinting in the sun. Threads of blue smoke rose from the huts into the morning air and people were moving about in their doorways and on their rickety verandas.

"*Home, nearly,*" announced Carlos, landing on a bush that wasn't really ready to take his weight. "*Home, nearly, nearly,*" he said again, bouncing on a whippy branch. "*Riverboat.*"

The sight of a skinny brown child, a fat

coati and a talking macaw wasn't at all unusual to the people of the village. They were mostly quite skinny and brown themselves, and wild jungle animals often became their pets. So they smiled as Dog walked between their homes with Esme trotting beside her and Carlos resting on her shoulder. They greeted her too, with words she'd never heard before, but which were somehow more familiar than the ones she'd heard every day in the pet shop.

"*Hola!*"

"*Qué pasa?*"

The words were even more familiar to Carlos. He greeted them back and even asked questions. "*Barco ría arriba?*" he said.

"*Cobetizo orilla,*" people told him.

It seemed perfectly ordinary to them that a macaw should ask where to get a boat upriver. That was where the macaws lived.

A wiry man with threads of grey in his hair and a neat moustache stood by a ramshackle boathouse. He wore an orange T-shirt, a voluminous pair of bright blue shorts and a faded baseball cap with the word AMAZONINO written on it. His boat was long and narrow, with faded pink paint and a little outboard motor at the back. It was already quite full of round drums of petrol, sacks of rice and woven

baskets with live chickens inside. He smiled and showed two perfect front teeth when he heard Carlos speak.

"Yes, I go upriver. You have money?" he said in Spanish.

"*Have money*," Carlos repeated in the same language.

"No money, I take the bird," said the man.

"*Take the bird*," Carlos said, copying the man's voice perfectly.

Dog didn't understand a word, but smiling and nodding had worked with Asky, so she tried it out again here. The man grinned back. Then he helped them into the boat and cast off. In just a few minutes the jetty was far behind and the boat was puttering its way up the wide river.

Chapter 25

They cruised steadily up the middle of the mouse-brown river. The man, whose name was Hoehe, sat at the back, lazily holding the tiller and smoking little cigarettes. Dog and her friends sat in the prow, jammed in front of two sacks of rice and a huge tin of marmalade. The sky was a hazy blue and the air streamed over them, cool and heavy.

Once or twice a day Hoehe stopped at villages, dropped off supplies, and collected passengers or small cargo and replenished their water supplies to carry to the next stop. People were interested in the child and her two companions. They gave them food, admired the bird and petted the coati but mostly left them to themselves, up there at the front of the boat.

At night Hoehe moored the boat at little jetties or small beaches. He caught fish and cooked it over a fire, but never offered to share it. Esme found her own food, scrabbling in the muddy banks as if she'd been doing it all her life. Carlos cracked Brazil nuts lying in the bottom of the boat. Dog mostly went hungry.

At first the banks on either side were so far away that they were just distant walls of bright green. Occasionally flocks of white birds erupted from sand banks, or the movement of some animal flickered between the bank and the water, too far away to see properly. But as the days went on, the river narrowed and the banks got closer. Now Dog could see huge trees, with dark dipping branches tangled in leaves and climbers. Flashes of brightly coloured wings showed in the treetops. Once they passed a muddy bank where huge caimans were sunning themselves. Uncle had once bought a tank of baby ones for the pet shop. Dog had loved them, but had almost lost a finger or two giving them their dinner!

She could understand why they had been so hungry if this was how much growing they had to do!

Esme, usually so ready for a snooze at any hour, hardly slept at all during the journey. She stood on the very prow of the bow, with her ears pricked and her nose pointing forward like a quivering compass needle. Dog could see she was soaking up every smell and sound and sight.

Carlos was excited too. He flapped his wings and even took off at times, circling the boat as if he wanted it to go faster. He seemed unable to be still for a moment. He said very little apart from mimicking Hoehe's terrible singing or the puttering of the outboard. But at night he kept Dog company. He perched next to where she slept on the sacks of rice, so close she could hear him breathing and smell his warm, dry feathers.

Dog could see a change coming over her friends. Esme's tail seemed stripier, despite the missing fur; Carlos's feathers more like sky and sunshine than ever before. The life of the river and the forest was beginning to flow through them. Dog felt it too. She was filled with a kind of fizzing sensation, a mixture of comfort and excitement. She felt as if all her insides had been arranged into new patterns and then lit up, like Asky's shiny sky-man, Orion.

Some nights Hoehe didn't sleep, so they kept on going all through the warm darkness. Dog slept in fits and starts, waking to stars dancing on the water, Esme reaching her nose into the breeze or Carlos spreading his wings to the moonlight.

Dog didn't count all the nights and days, but at last, one evening, when the sun dipped behind the trees, Hoehe steered his *baraca* up to a little jetty, where a cluster of grassy huts gathered on the river bank. Hoehe tied the boat up and pointed to a worn notice on a pole:

ZEE FOUNDATION MAOHURI RESERVE, it announced. ADMISSION STRICTLY BY PERMIT ONLY.

"I can't go any further," he said. "You're a Maohuri, aren't you, so you can get out here."

Dog smiled and nodded, but of course she couldn't read the notice. She understood, though, that this was the end of their journey.

Stiffly she unfolded herself and, with Carlos on her shoulder and Esme at her feet, got ready to climb out of the boat. She stared about, feeling that this was the strangest, and also the most familiar place she had been. The forest pressed in all around them, dense and huge and green, as if the trees had just stepped back a little so the huts could stand. The air was soft and moist, full of scents and the sounds of insects, frogs, birds.

But Hoehe didn't let the little waif stare about her in that dazed way for long. He wanted his payment. It was obvious now that the child had no money and he was looking forward to the fat price that a talking macaw would make back in town.

"Where's my money?" he said in Spanish.

Dog smiled and nodded, but Hoehe wasn't smiling any more. He was tired now, and cross. He decided could probably sell the scrappy old coati too – and the girl, if it came to it.

"Where's my *money?*" He stepped up to Dog and stood over her, looking much bigger and less wiry than he had seemed before. Suddenly Hoehe's intentions were very clear. Dog knew all the signs – she'd learned them from Uncle. She felt small and sick. She hung her head and trembled. Esme climbed into her arms, chittering in fear, and hid her face in her tail.

Carlos stood on Dog's shoulder and flapped his wings. "*No money,*" he said in Hoehe's voice. "*No money.*"

Hoehe's face froze. "OK," he said, "then I *take* my payment." He snatched up a big black box from the bottom of the boat in one hand, and Dog's wrist in the other. "Give me the bird or I will kill your coati and slice out your heart and feed it to the piranhas. I've had plenty of birds and children in this box. You won't be the first or the last!"

Dog didn't understand the words, but she could see their meaning very clearly. Hoehe held the black box open. Inside were feathers of all colours – blue and gold like Carlos's own, scarlet, green, even deep violet. There were signs of humans too – tiny hand prints and the marks of scraping nails.

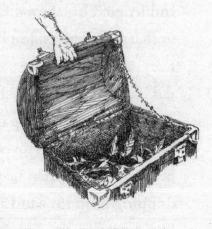

There would be no escape for any of them, even for clever Carlos, from that box.

Dog was very, very afraid, but she had not come so far for a box like Uncle's to swallow her or her friends at last. With all her strength she kicked the black, black box, and it spun from Hoehe's hand, over the side, and sank. At the same moment Esme reached out from behind her tail to sink her teeth into the hand that held Dog's wrist. Hoehe yelped in pain and let go. Dog shoved Carlos off her shoulder so that he could fly, leaped onto the jetty with Esme and ran.

Hoehe had been sure his bullying would work on this little scrap of a girl. So it took him a moment to recover from the surprise of her sheer cheek; then he was after her, blood dripping from his hand as he gathered speed. His strong boatman's legs worked like pistons,

and his moustache set in a determined line. If he couldn't catch the bird, he was sure he could catch the girl.

Dog ran up the jetty and straight into the middle of the village, between the little huts made of wooden poles and grass. Something about the place made her feel instantly safer, more certain that she could escape.

People like those in Marmalade's photo stood in doorways or lazed in hammocks, and they all turned to watch the little girl run by with her coati at her ankles. Not such a strange sight, but the gold and blue macaw screeching just above her head was a bit unusual.

On she ran, with Esme panting beside her and Carlos circling above, but Hoehe had longer legs. Just where the village turned again to jungle, he caught her. He clamped one hand in her hair and dragged her back towards the river.

Carlos yelled and dived-bombed him. Esme snarled and slashed at his legs with her claws and teeth.

Now Hoehe was really angry. He shook the brat, wanting to pull out her hair by its miserable Maohuri roots. He kicked and waved his free arm to try and ward off the bird, but Carlos was devilishly clever at avoiding his blows.

The villagers rushed towards the commotion, their curiosity aroused. Hoehe found his way back to the river blocked, as every family had come out to see what was going on.

"So," said Moipa, the village head man, in Spanish, "what's all the fuss?"

"Step aside, Indian scum," said Hoehe (who was sure that he was descended from the Spanish conquistadors).

The villagers had never much cared for Hoehe – he always overcharged them for goods transported up the river – so his lack of manners drew even more attention. They closed in around him a little more: they didn't like the way he was holding onto the child, who looked just like one of their own, or the way he had hit out at her animals.

"I think you should let this child

go," said Moipa.

"Child? She's a thief. She tricked me. I brought her upriver because she said she'd pay me with that bird." Hoehe pointed to Carlos, still trying to dive-bomb him.

Moipa turned to Dog. "Is this true?"

But Dog didn't answer.

"It's no good asking her," Hoehe grumbled. "She's a mute!"

"But you said she *told* you she would give you the bird," said Moipa.

"Yes," added his wife, Akawo. "How did she do that if she's a mute?"

Hoehe opened and closed his mouth like a landed piranha. He let go of Dog's hair, and she dropped to the floor beside Esme. Carlos swooped down onto her shoulder, and Esme sat at her feet.

"*Give me the bird*," said Carlos, in Hoehe's

voice, "*or I will kill your coati and slice out your heart and feed it to the piranhas. I've had plenty of birds and children in this box.*"

Horrified gasps and murmurs spread throughout the crowd – which was now almost everyone in the village.

"I see," said Moipa. "I think you'd better go, and never come back."

"Yes!" added the villagers. "Go!"

"You don't have a permit to be here anyway!" added Akawo.

Hoehe shook his fist and crossed himself, then he turned and fled. Esme chased him, snarling, her bandaged tail up, all the way back to the river.

Chapter 26

The arrival of the girl with the powerful animal companions seemed like a very good omen to the villagers. Although she looked like a child of their own tribe, she seemed rather strange, so they spoke to her, not in their own language, but in their very best and most respectful Spanish. They led her to a guest hut close to a little beach, and brought her food and lit her fire for her. Then they left her in peace.

Dog was in a daze. The shape of the huts, the smell of the cooking fires, the faces of the people, even the sounds of frogs and insects that came from the forest as night fell were somehow things she knew, like the parts of a dream she couldn't quite remember. With Esme curled beside her, and Carlos roosting on a perch nearby, Dog lay down to sleep.

At first light, she stoked the fire to wake it up, and the three friends shared the food the villagers had brought them. Dog watched the sun rise over the trees and make a shining path on the river. Esme got bored with the view and started rooting about on the bank, looking for something juicy and alive for dessert.

Carlos came and perched beside Dog on a log next to the fire. He bent his head towards her, delicately raising all his neck feathers. "*Scratch,*" he cooed softly. "*Scratch.*"

Very carefully, Dog scratched the dry white skin between the soft feathers. Carlos closed his eyes and purred. "*Home,*" he said quietly.

"*Home. All home.*" Then he smoothed his
feathers flat, and looked intently into Dog's
face with his strange eyes, each one in turn,
then both together, over the curve of his beak.
"*Goodbye,*" he said. "*Goodbye.*"

And then he was gone. He flew straight over

the water to where a flock of macaws just like
him were flapping upstream. Dog watched as
Carlos drew closer and closer to them. Then,
quite suddenly, he was among them, no longer
separate and "Carlos" but a part of the flock. A
moment later, their calls and colours were lost
in the green of the forest.

Dog cried as she had never cried before. She cried because Carlos had gone, and because she too wanted a flock to fly with. She cried because Carlos had lent her a voice, and now that he was gone, she had none.

But she understood. Carlos had to be what he had never been before: a macaw amongst other macaws. He would not be coming back.

She sat there all morning and into the afternoon, staring at the river. Esme brought her three green beetles and a small yellow frog to try and cheer her up, but it didn't work.

The sun set, turning the river the colour of blood and flowers. At last Dog stopped crying. She watched the darkness rise up with all the stars studded into it. She breathed in the warm softness of the air, and the night sounds of the forest, then she curled up beside Esme, and slept.

A voice came into Dog's dreams. A child's voice that burst into her mind like shafts of light into a darkened room.

Dog's eyes shot open. It wasn't a dream. Someone was coming through the forest towards her. It was the head man's son, who was too young to be bothered with Spanish, so he called out greetings in the language of the village, the language that had grown from the river and the forest as naturally and easily as the trees and the fishes.

Dog's heart raced. She knew these words – knew them in a way she'd never known the words that Uncle spoke. Inside her silent heart, words rose up like a country rising from the sea. The dream-like blur of the huts, the river, the great trees, shimmered into focus, and a memory, a real memory of a time before Uncle, grew inside her like a bright bubble.

She remembered a beach by a river, just like this. She remembered the light on the water, the dry warmth of her mother's arms around her, the safe smell of her mother's skin and the line of blue parrots against the green. Her mother's voice had whispered – whispered words that named the trees, the water, the birds and herself!

The boy stepped out from under the trees into the clearing where the guest hut stood. He had been away from the village for a few days and hadn't seen their visitor. "Hello," he said, a little surprised to find a child rather like himself. "Who are you?"

The answer was in Dog's heart, where her mother had put it. In a voice so tiny it seemed to come from far away, Dog spoke.

"I'm named after the blue macaw," she said. "I'm called Mintak."

About the author . . .

Nicola Davies graduated from Cambridge with a degree in zoology before going on to become a writer and presenter of radio and television programmes such as THE REALLY WILD SHOW. Amongst her many acclaimed books for children are *Big Blue Whale*, *One Tiny Turtle*, *Ice Bear*, *Extreme Animals* and *Poo*, which was shortlisted for a Blue Peter Book Award. Her novel *Home* was shortlisted for the Branford Boase award.

Dog

The first time I saw Dog in my head, I imagined looking down on her through a skylight window on a frosty night. There she was, curled up in a dog bed with a coati whom I immediately recognized as Esme, my old friend from Sparkwell Wildlife Park.

I knew what Dog looked like right from the

start: dusty-brown skin, thick black hair and deep, deep brown eyes set in a wide face. I knew where she came from too – somewhere in the Amazon Rainforest, in South America. Later I read more about native people from remote regions of the Amazon, and that was where I found Dog's real name – which we find out right at the end of the story.

At the time I began writing *A Girl Called Dog*, I'd been reading about how slavery, especially child slavery, is still happening all over the world. I read about children stolen from their families and taken thousands of miles away to work for nothing as servants, on farms and in factories. I read about orphaned children, with no one to protect or care for them, treated like objects that could be bought, sold and thrown away. Dog grew out of all I'd learned about these powerless children exploited by adults who are supposed to know better. I imagined Dog to be a young girl stolen from her family and put to work in Uncle's pet shop, like so many children in the world that this really happens to.

Dog grew out of something else, too. All my life I've been aware of how the world's rainforests are being destroyed – cut down for their wood, and plundered for their valuable wildlife and natural resources. Some of the first stories I worked on as a young TV researcher were about the illegal trade in South American cat skins – jaguar and ocelot – and the importation of exotic parrot species for the pet trade. I saw photos of boxes stuffed with spotted skins from hundreds of rare cats, and of suitcases full of live parrots, packed in so tightly that many of them suffocated on their journey. For me, Dog's situation – being stolen from the Amazon, that fabulous treasure of natural wonders – became a symbol for all that destruction.

There was one other thing that contributed

to Dog's character, and that's the ability of children living in poverty, danger and deprivation to still smile and play. Dog has had a terrible start in life, and yet she can still feel lucky and positive. She has a quiet strength about her and I only found out where that came from right at the end of the book . . . but I won't give that away in case you haven't read it yet!

Esme the coati

(Pronounced co-are-tee)

Of all the characters I've ever written about, Esme is the one closest to reality. Years ago I presented the *Birthday Requests Show* for West Country TV. The best thing about that job was that I had regular contact with animals from the local wildlife park, Sparkwell. One of viewers' favourite animals – and mine too – was a ringtailed coati called Esme.

Coatis are South American relatives of racoons; they have long, turned-up noses, even longer stripy tails and dextrous paws with claws that look like elegant fingernails – well, they do to me, anyway! Coati females are very sociable and live in big bands of mothers and babies, sharing food and helping each other out. They are good climbers but mostly live on the forest floor where their snuffly noses and clever claws winkle out anything edible – insects, roots, bird eggs, lizards, mice, fruit and nuts. Coatis are often taken as pets by native people who live in the forest, and being clever and liking company, coatis settle in well with human families.

The real Esme, like the Esme in this book, was pretty old when I got to know her, with fur thinning on her stripy tail and bald patches on her body. We just took to each other immediately and whenever we met, Esme would climb onto my shoulders and push her nose under my hair. I absolutely adored her and it didn't surprise me that she turned up here, years later, as Dog's best friend.

Carlos the macaw

I've always been fascinated by animals that can talk. The idea that a human could have a real conversation with an animal enthrals me.

Children's books are full of 'talking' animals, but to me, they usually seem less like real animals and more like humans in animal costumes. In reality, most talking animals are really just very clever mimics, copying human sounds and gestures without understanding their meaning. However, while I was doing the research for a book about animal communication, I found some famous exceptions. One was a chimp called Washoe, who was raised by humans and learned human sign language – chimps don't have the right vocal chords or tongues for speech. Washoe 'talked' to her human carers and to other chimps in the human sign language she'd learned, and even taught another chimp to sign without human help.

The other example was Alex the African grey parrot. African greys are well-known for their ability to mimic sounds, including human voices and words, but Alex wasn't just a copycat. He used the words he learned to answer questions, showing that he understood their meaning, and even made up sentences on his own. I was very excited when I heard about Alex and the things he said to his human friend Dr Irene Pepperberg, including the last words he ever spoke to her: 'I love you'.

Dr Pepperberg's work with Alex showed me that it *was* possible for humans and animals to really talk, so I *could* have an animal character whose communication with humans was real, not magical. I was careful when I wrote Carlos's speech to keep it within the bounds of what a real parrot like Alex might have managed.

I did stretch reality by making Carlos a blue and gold macaw, as they aren't particularly good mimics; but I needed a parrot from the Amazon and, as a little girl, I'd dreamed of having a pet blue and gold macaw that would fly freely into the trees but come to me when I called. So Carlos was my dream come true!

As the story progressed, I thought more about Carlos and the life he had led among humans. Would he long to be just a normal parrot once again? I understood, in the end, that both Dog and Carlos were making a journey to discover their true selves. Esme too was going home, but for Esme, home was always going to be just where Dog was.

A Girl Called Dog is a fictional story, but its roots are in the real world, and run deep into my life and my own heart. I hope that makes it strong, and able to speak to everyone who reads it.

Nicola

Have you read these other
fantastic animal tales?

*A very hairy tale by the bestselling,
award-winning Dick King-Smith*

HAIRY HEZEKIAH

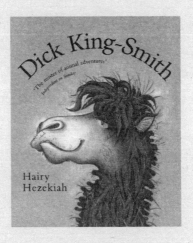

Hezekiah is a very hairy camel. He lives a quiet life
in his enclosure at the zoo and seems to be the only
animal without a friend.

So Hezekiah decides to escape from the zoo
and go on the run – crashing through hedges,
hiding in toilets, and breaking into a safari park!
There he meets another hairy creature –
and finally makes a friend . . .

An exciting story from Whitbread Award-winning author Michael Morpurgo

TOM'S SAUSAGE LION

'But it's true,' Tom shouted. 'It was a real lion, I know it was.'

No one believes Tom when he says he has seen a lion strolling through the orchard with a string of sausages dangling from its mouth! No one, that is, apart from Clare – the cleverest girl in his class. Together, Tom and Clare hatch a daring plan to prove they are telling the truth . . .

A thrilling tale from Whitbread and Carnegie-winning author Philip Pullman

I WAS A RAT!
or *The Scarlet Slippers*

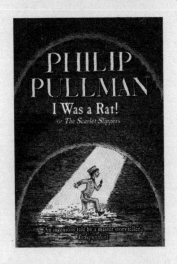

When a small boy turns up on Bob and Joan's doorstep unable to say much except 'I was a rat!', the kind couple adopt him. Roger tries very hard to adapt to human life – but when he gets lost and ends up on the run, people start to say he's the Monster, a rodent fiend who could terrorise the town.
Only one person can save Roger now . . .